STORMY WEATHER

Amanda Harvey

Lothrop, Lee & Shepard Books
New York

To Rachel and Helen

First U.S. Edition 1992 1 2 3 4 5 6 7 8 9 10

Library of Congress Cataloging in Publication Data
Harvey, Amanda. Stormy weather / Amanda Harvey.
p.   cm. Summary: Winter approaches as Maud and Mrs. Perkins go blackberrying. ISBN 0-688-10607-2. —
ISBN 0-688-10608-0 (lib. bdg.) [1. Winter—Fiction.] I. Title. PZ7.H26745St 1992 [E]—dc20 91-13950 CIP AC

Maud walked into the kitchen.
She sat at the table, and poured herself some cereal,

which she had started to eat

when she heard a knock at the window
and saw Mrs. Perkins inviting her out.

Together they walked through the village

and across the fields to the woods.

"Blackberries," said Mrs. Perkins, stopping at a bramble.
"I could eat them forever."

"Yes," said Maud, "but you have to watch out for the
prickles," and they stood blackberrying quietly under
the trees.

Then, very faintly at first, they heard strange singing in
the distance, and the leaves began to rustle.

"That sounds like Winter," said Mrs. Perkins, surprised.

They hid behind a tree and watched as Winter appeared
with his rake. Now they could clearly hear the words of
his chilly song:

> *"I blow on leaf and fruit and vine*
> *and bring with me the change of time.*
> *So where the bee sucked, there breathe I,*
> *and where I tread a bloom will die."*

Sometimes he would break off from his song, blow on the leaves until they fell, and push them aside with his rake. Then he would start again:

> *"I take the Autumn leaves away,*
> *and in their place a carpet lay*
> *of dank and dark and bitter cold*
> *to freeze . . ."*

"We must stop him," whispered Maud.

"Oh no!" said Mrs. Perkins. "We wouldn't be able to do that."

But Maud couldn't bear to see such ruin and ran forward shouting, "Stop!"

Winter paused. He looked at Maud out of the
corner of his eye and then he blew purposefully
on the leaves, causing a great turmoil.

"No," cried Maud, "you must stop!" and she tried to bar his way. But Winter threw back his head and laughed, then pushed past and went on down the path, raking the trees bare to left and right.

At the end of the wood he turned and called back: "Time rolls on, child – time rolls on . . ." and singing loudly, he faded into the distance.

"Now Winter's here and Autumn's passed,
no berries left – time's change was fast . . ."

"Well," said Mrs. Perkins, "that's that."
"Yes," sighed Maud, touching the shriveled bushes, "but not forever."
"No," said Mrs. Perkins, "not forever."

"He thinks he's so clever," said Maud as they walked back,
"but we have a whole cupboard full of blackberries
at home."

Later that evening, Maud took a jar of
berries off the shelf, which they made up into
a pie for supper.